A GIFT FOR:

_____

FROM:

_____

Story time and play time are a lot more fun when You're the Star!

Here's how it works:

Story time

1. Put on the cape and secure it around your shoulders.
2. Turn the device to **ON** using the switch located on its side.
3. Press the front of the device one time to begin **story time!**

- *When an adult reads the highlighted phrases in the book, you'll hear action-packed sounds and responses.*

Play time

1. Put on the cape and secure it around your shoulders.
2. Turn the device to **ON** using the switch located on its side.
3. Press the front of the device two times to begin **play time!**

- *Say the trigger phrases listed in the back of each book to hear even more magical sounds and to make play time even more fun!*

Collect all of the Batgirl books to find out more magical phrases!

TM & © DC Comics.
(s14)

Mfd. for Hallmark Marketing, LLC
Kansas City, MO 64141
Produced in China
Visit us on the Web at Hallmark.com.

Editorial Director: Carrie Bolin
Editors: Megan Langford and Nate Barbarick
Art Director: Jan Mastin
Designer: Scott Swanson
Production Designer: Dan Horton
Music Composer/Sound Designer: Chris Johnson

ISBN: 978-1-59530-673-9
KOB8111

Printed and bound in China
MAY14

BATGIRL

AND THE PLANTS OF PERIL!

By Andrew Blackburn

Illustrated by Josh Holtsclaw

Hallmark

Batgirl couldn't believe her eyes. Right in the middle of Gotham City—something big. Something crazy. Something . . . flowery?

"We have no idea what's going on here, Batgirl," Commissioner Gordon said. "But we need your help to figure it out."

"No problem," Batgirl said. "We'll find the flower-crazy villain behind all this."

Batgirl examined the giant flower, when suddenly . . . **WHOOSH!** Batgirl yanked Commissioner Gordon out of the way. Giant plants had started springing up all over the place!

"Thank you, Batgirl! That was close," said Commissioner Gordon. "We'd better figure out what's going on, and fast."

"I'm on it, Commissioner," said Batgirl. "Saving the day is what I do best."

Batgirl jumped on her motorcycle and zoomed off. She swerved through giant trees, skidded around huge bushes, weaved through enormous flowers . . . this jungle was taking over the city!

Then, something dangling from a high tree branch caught her eye. But it wasn't a plant. It was a person!

Batgirl jumped into the tree.

"Help me! I'm slipping!" the man shouted.
Batgirl pulled out her grappling hook and fired away! She
swung upward and grabbed the man out of the tree. And
just as she did . . .

CRAACK!
The branch tumbled to the ground.

"Thanks, Batgirl!" the man said.
"You're welcome," said Batgirl.
"But maybe hold off on any more
tree climbing for a while."

Things were getting crazy in Gotham City, so Batgirl headed to the Batcave to figure out what was going on. Batgirl shouted, "Batcomputer, activate!"

POISON IVY

LIVE

WAYNE

GCN   WAYNE TOWER

A news program popped up on the screen. And there was the criminal—Poison Ivy! She was right there on camera, standing on top of Wayne Tower. Now Batgirl knew who was responsible for all this mayhem—and where to find her!

Batgirl jumped on her motorcycle and zoomed off! She made her way to Wayne Tower. But the plants were so thick, she couldn't make it to the building! Batgirl knew there was only one way to go—straight up!

WHOOSH! Just as Batgirl stepped onto the rooftop, a giant apple whizzed by her head. Straight ahead was the biggest apple tree she had ever seen! Batgirl flung her Batarang through the air.

The world's biggest apples were about to become the world's biggest fruit salad!

One false move and she'd fall straight to those giant chompers! Batgirl pulled out her grappling hook and fired away! She made it! Now she was ready to face off against Poison Ivy.

Poison Ivy was ready for Batgirl. "You may have gotten by my plants," she said. "But you'll never get me!"

WHOOSH!

SWISH! Two giant vines shot at Batgirl, trying to wrap her up! "You're just an overgrown weed that needs to be pulled!" Batgirl shouted back.

"You saved our city again, Batgirl," said Commissioner Gordon. "You're a true hero."
"It was nothing, Commissioner," Batgirl said. "After all, saving the day is what I do best!"

Turn the page for more fun with BATGIRL

Press the medallion one more time, then try saying
these phrases when you're out playing!

Time to save the day!

Ready or not, here I come!

I'll get you, Catwoman!

Batcomputer, activate!

See how you like my Batarang!

Ready, aim, fire!

I've got you now!

You're mine, Poison Ivy!

If you had fun reading this boo
we would love to hear from yo

Please send your comments t
Hallmark Book Feedback
P.O. Box 419034
Mail Drop 100
Kansas City, MO 64141

Or e-mail us at:
booknotes@hallmark.com